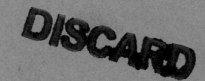

The Complete Story of the
Three Blind Mice

by John W. Ivimey
Illustrated by Paul Galdone

CLARION BOOKS
TICKNOR & FIELDS: A HOUGHTON MIFFLIN COMPANY
NEW YORK

Clarion Books
Ticknor & Fields, A Houghton Mifflin Company
Illustrations copyright © 1987 by the Estate of Paul Galdone

Library of Congress Cataloging-in-Publication Data
Ivimey, John W. (John William), 1868-
The complete story of The Three blind mice.

Originally published: Complete version of ye three
blind mice.
Summary: Three small mice in search of fun become
hungry, scared, blind, wise, and, finally, happy.
[1. Mice—Fiction.   2. Stories in rhyme]
I. Galdone, Paul, ill.   II. Ivimey, John W. (John William),
1868-   . Complete version of ye three blind
mice.   III. Three blind mice.   IV. Title.
PZ8.3I83Co   1987   [E]   87-689
ISBN 0-89919-481-8

Y   10   9   8   7   6   5   4   3   2   1

Three small mice

Three small mice
Wished for some fun
Wished for some fun

They made up their minds
to set out to roam,
Said they,
"'Tis dull to remain at home,"

And all the luggage they took was a comb,
These three small mice.

Three bold mice
Three bold mice
    Came to an inn
    Came to an inn
"Good evening host,
can you give us a bed?"

But the host just grinned and shook his head,

So they all slept out in the field instead,
These three bold mice.

Three cold mice
Three cold mice
        Woke up next morn
        Woke up next morn

They each had a cold and a swollen face,
From sleeping all night in an open space,

So they rose quite early and left the place,
These three cold mice.

Three hungry mice
Three hungry mice
      Searched for some food
      Searched for some food

But all they found was a walnut shell
That lay by the side of a dried-up well.
Who had eaten the nut they could not tell,
These three hungry mice.

Three starved mice
Three starved mice
    Came to a farm
    Came to a farm

The farmer was eating some bread and cheese,
So they all went down on their hands and knees,

And squeaked, "Oh give us a morsel please,"
These three starved mice.

Three glad mice
Three glad mice
Ate all they could
Ate all they could

They felt so happy they danced with glee,
But the farmer's wife came in to see
What might this merry-making be,
Of three glad mice.
    Three poor mice
    Three poor mice
        Soon changed their tone
        Soon changed their tone

The farmer's wife said, "What are you at?
And why are you prancing around like that?

Just you wait,
I'll fetch the cat.
You naughty,
naughty mice."

Three scared mice
Three scared mice
        Ran for their lives
        Ran for their lives

The mention of "Cat" set their teeth on edge,
So they jumped out onto the window ledge,

And made a leap for the bramble hedge,
These three scared mice.

Three sad mice
Three sad mice
What could they do
What could they do

The bramble hedge was most unkind,
It scratched their eyes and made them blind,

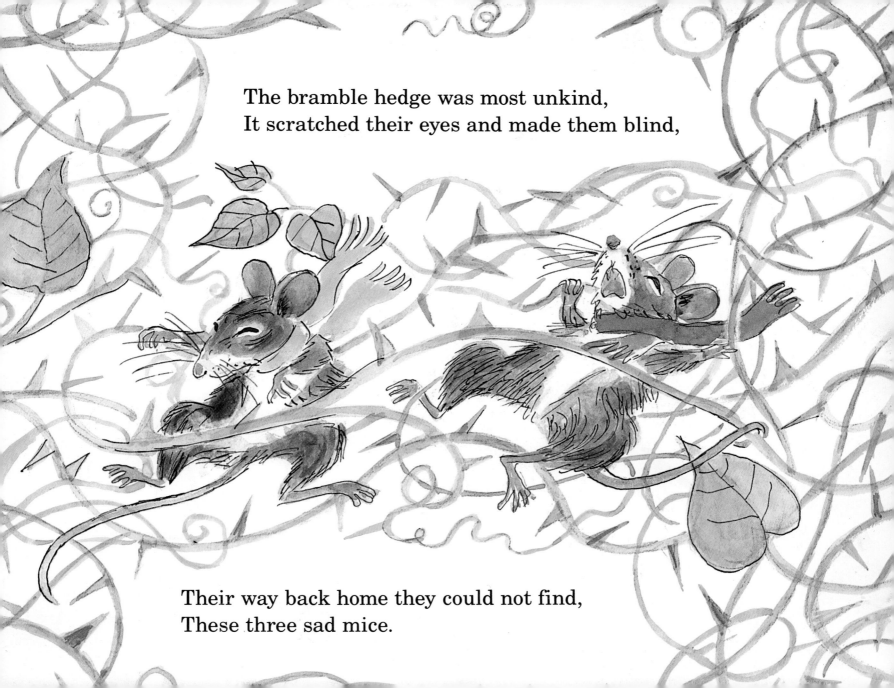

Their way back home they could not find,
These three sad mice.

Three blind mice
Three blind mice
    See how they run
    See how they run
They all ran after the farmer's wife,
Who cut off their tails with a carving knife,

Did you ever see such a sight in your life,
As three blind mice?

Three sick mice
Three sick mice
    Gave way to tears
    Gave way to tears
They could not see, and they had no end,
They hoped for magic, then found a friend,
He gave them some "Never Too Late To Mend,"
These three sick mice.

Three wise mice
Three wise mice
    Rubbed rubbed away
    Rubbed rubbed away

And soon their tails began to grow,
And their eyes recovered their sight, you know,

They looked in the pond and it told them so,

These three wise mice.

Three happy mice
Three happy mice
    Soon settled down
    Soon settled down

They built a house,
so I hear tell,
Each learned a trade
and is doing well,

If you call upon them, ring the bell,
Three times twice.